Two Old Women

An Alaska Legend
of Betrayal, Courage
and Survival

Two Old Women

. . . .

An Alaska Legend
of Betrayal, Courage and Survival

By VELMA WALLIS
Illustrations by Jim Grant

EPICENTER PRESS
Alaska Book Adventures™
www.EpicenterPress.com

Epicenter Press is a regional press founded in Alaska whose interests include but are not limited to the arts, history, environment, and diverse cultures and lifestyles of the Pacific Northwest and high latitudes. We seek both the traditional and innovative in publishing nonfiction books, and contemporary art and photography gift books.

Publisher: Kent Sturgis
Acquisition Editor: Lael Morgan
Editors: Virginia Sims, Kent Sturgis
Proofreader: Susan Ohrberg
Reading group discussion guide: Mick Craker
Researcher: Polly Wheeler
Cover and book design: Leslie Newman, Newman Design/Illustration
Printer: Transcontinental Printing

Library of Congress Control Number 2004104023
ISBN 0-9724944-9-9

Booksellers: This title is available from our trade distributor, Graphic Arts Center Publishing Co., PO Box 10306, Portland, OR 97210, call 800-452-3032 or visit www.gacpc.com. *Wholesale discounts are available.*

PRINTED IN CANADA

Second Edition, May 2004
First Edition, September 1993, published by Epicenter Press Inc.

10 9 8 7 6 5 4 3 2 1

To order single copies of TWO OLD WOMEN *mail $17.95 plus $6.95 for shipping and handling (WA residents add $2.20 state sales tax) to: Epicenter Press, PO Box 82368, Kenmore, WA 98028.*

Discover exciting ALASKA BOOK ADVENTURES™! Visit our online Alaska bookstore at www.EpicenterPress.com or call our 24-hour, toll-free hotline at 800-950-6663. Visit our online gallery featuring one of Alaska's favorite artists, Jon Van Zyle, www.JonVanZyle.com.

Table of Contents

Dedication. vii

Acknowledgements ix

Introduction xi

CHAPTER 1: Hunger and cold take their toll . . . 1

CHAPTER 2: "Let us die trying". 17

CHAPTER 3: Recalling old skills 29

CHAPTER 4: A painful journey 43

MAP . . . . 70 - 71

CHAPTER 5: Saving a cache of fish 73

CHAPTER 6: Sadness among The People 87

CHAPTER 7: The stillness is broken 99

CHAPTER 8: A new beginning. 113

About the Gwich'in People 127

Editor's Afterword 131

Book Club Discussion Guide 137

Dedication

This book is dedicated to all of the elders whom I have known and who have made an impression in my mind with their wisdom, knowledge and uniqueness.

Mae P. Wallis, Mary Hardy, Dorothy Earls, Sarah Gottschalk, Ida Neyhart, Patricia Peters, Edison Peters, Helen Reed, Moses Peter, Martha Wallis, Louise Paul, Minnie Salmon, Lilly Herbert, David and Sarah Salmon, Samson and Minnie Peter, Herbert and Louise Peter, Stanley and Rosalie Joseph, Margaret John, Paul and Margaret Williams, Leah Roberts, Natalie Erick, Daniel Horace, Titus Peter, Solomon and Martha Flitt, Doris Ward, Amos Kelly, Margaret Kelly, Maggie Beach, Sarah Alexander, Peter and Nina (Chidzigyaak) Joseph, Paul and Agnes James, Mariah Collins, David Collins, Mary Thompson, Sophie Williams, Elijah John, Jemima Fields, Ike Fields Sr., Joe and Margaret Carroll, Myra Francis, Blanche Strom, Arthur and Annie

James, Elliot and Lucy Johnson, Elliot and Virginia Johnson II,

Harry and Jessie Carroll, Margaret Cadzow, Henry and Jennie Williams, Issac and Sarah John, Charlotte Douthit, Ruth Martin, Randall Baalam, Harold and Ester Petersen, Vladimer and Nina Petersen, Addie Shewfelt, Stanley and Madeline Jonas, Jonathon and Hannah Solomon, Esau and Delia Williams, Margie Englishoe, Jessie Luke, Julia Peter, Jacob Flitt, Daniel and Nina Flitt, Clara Gundrum, Jessie Williams, Sarah W. John, Mary Simple, Ellen Henry, Silas John, Dan Frank, Maggie Roberts, Nina Roberts, Abraham and Annie Christian, Paul and Julia Tritt, Agnes Peter, Charlie Peter, Neil and Sarah Henry, Mardow Solomon, Ruth Peterson, Phillip and Abbie Peter,

Archie and Louise Juneby, Harry and Bessie David, Margaret Roberts, John Stevens, Steven and Sarah Henry, Abel Tritt, Moses and Jennie Sam, Mary John, Martha James, Alice Peter, Nathanial and Annie Frank, Fred and Charlotte Thomas, Richard and Eva Carroll, Elsie Pitka, Richard and Helen Martin, Paul Gabrial, Grafton Gabrial, Barbara Solomon, Sabastian McGinty, Simon and Bella Francis, Mary Jane Alexander, and Uncle Lee Henry.

Acknowledgements

Most artists can say that if it were not for a number of people he or she would not have achieved a certain success. In the case of this story and myself, the list is long and varied and I would like to acknowledge them as follows.

First, thank you to my mother, Mae Wallis. Without you, this story would not be, and I never would have developed a desire to be a storyteller. All those many nights that you spent telling us stories are greatly appreciated.

I would like to thank these people for believing in this story all these years, and for reviving it just when I thought it would sink back into oblivion: Barry Wallis, Marti Ann Wallis, Patricia Stanley, and Carroll Hodge; Judy Erick from Venetie for her flexible assistance with the Gwich'in translations and Annette Seimens for letting me use her computer.

Last, I would like to thank Marilyn Savage for her generosity and persistent rallying. Thank you to

Acknowledgements

the publishers, Kent Sturgis and Lael Morgan, for sharing the same vision as all of us. Thank you to Virigina Sims for making sure that the story remained the same with your editing, and to James Grant for making the characters come to life with your talented illustrations.

Mahsi Choo to each and all of you for sharing in this humble story.

Velma

Introduction

Each day after cutting wood we would sit and talk in our small tent on the bank at the mouth of the Porcupine River, near where it flows into the Yukon. We would always end with Mom telling me a story. (There I was, long past my youth, and my mother still told me bedtime stories!) One night it was a story I heard for the first time — a story about two old women and their journey through hardship.

What brought the story to mind was a conversation we had earlier while working side by side collecting wood for the winter. Now we sat on our bedrolls and marveled at how Mom in her early fifties still was able to do this kind of hard work while most people of her generation long since had resigned themselves to old age and all of its limitations. I told her I wanted to be like her when I became an elder.

We began to remember how it once was. My grandmother and all those other elders from the past kept themselves busy until they could no longer move or until they died. Mom felt proud that she was able to overcome some of the obstacles of old age and still could get her own winter wood despite the fact that physically, the work was difficult and sometimes agonizing. During our pondering and reflections, Mom remembered this particular story because it was appropriate to all that we thought and felt at that moment.

Later, at our winter cabin, I wrote the story down. I was impressed with it because it not only taught me a lesson that I could use in my life, but also because it was a story about my people and my past — something about me that I could grasp and call mine. Stories are gifts given by an elder to a younger person. Unfortunately, this gift is not given, nor received, as often today because many of our youth are occupied by television and the fast pace of modern-day living. Maybe tomorrow a few of today's generation who were sensitive enough to have listened to their elders' wisdom will have the traditional word-of-mouth stories living within their memory. Perhaps tomorrow's generation also will yearn for stories such as this so that they may better understand their past, their people and, hopefully, themselves.

Sometimes, too, stories told about one culture by someone from another way of life are misinterpreted. This is tragic. Once set down on paper, some stories are readily accepted as history, yet they may not be truthful.

This story of the two old women is from a time long before the arrival of the Western culture, and has been handed down from generation to generation, from person to person, to my mother, and then to me. Although I am writing it, using a little of my own creative imagination, this is, in fact, the story I was told and the point of the story remains the way Mom meant for me to hear it.

This story told me that there is no limit to one's ability — certainly not age — to accomplish in life what one must. Within each individual on this large and complicated world there lives an astounding potential of greatness. Yet it is rare that these hidden gifts are brought to life unless by the chance of fate.

CHAPTER 1
Hunger and cold take their toll

The air stretched tight, quiet and cold over the vast land. Tall spruce branches hung heavily laden with snow, awaiting distant spring winds. The frosted willows seemed to tremble in the freezing temperatures.

Far off in this seemingly dismal land were bands of people dressed in furs and animal skins, huddled close to small campfires. Their weather-burnt faces were stricken with looks of hopelessness as they faced starvation, and the future held little promise of better days.

These nomads were The People of the arctic region of Alaska, always on the move in search of food. Where the caribou and other migrating animals roamed, The People followed. But the deep cold of winter presented special problems. The moose, their favorite source of food, took refuge from the penetrating cold by staying in one place, and were difficult to find. Smaller, more accessible animals such as rabbits and tree squirrels could not sustain a large band such as this one. And during the cold spells, even the smaller animals either disappeared in hiding or were thinned by predators, man and animal alike. So during this unusually bitter chill in the late fall, the land seemed void of life as the cold hovered menacingly.

During the cold, hunting required more energy than at other times. Thus, the hunters were fed first, as it was their skills on which The People depended. Yet, with so many to feed, what food they had was depleted quickly. Despite their best efforts, many of the women and children suffered from malnutrition, and some would die of starvation.

In this particular band were two old women cared for by The People for many years. The older woman's name was Ch'idzigyaak, for she reminded her parents of a chickadee bird when she was born. The other woman's name was Sa', meaning "star," because at the time of her birth her mother had been looking at the fall night sky, concentrating on the distant stars to take her mind away from the painful labor contractions.

The chief would instruct the younger men to set up shelters for these two old women each time the band arrived at a new campsite, and to provide them with wood and water. The younger women pulled the two elder women's possessions from one camp to the next and, in turn, the old women tanned animal skins for those who helped them. The arrangement worked well.

However, the two old women shared a character flaw unusual for people of those times. Constantly they complained of aches and pains, and they carried walking sticks to attest to their handicaps. Surprisingly, the others seemed not to mind, despite having been taught from the days of their childhood that weakness was not tolerated among the inhabitants of this harsh motherland. Yet, no one reprimanded the two women, and they continued to travel with the stronger ones — until one fateful day.

On that day, something more than the cold hung in the air as The People gathered around their few flickering fires and listened to the chief. He was a man who stood almost a head taller than the other men. From within the folds of his parka ruff he spoke about the cold, hard days they were to expect and of what each would have to contribute if they were to survive the winter.

Then, in a loud, clear voice he made a sudden announcement: "The council and I have arrived at a decision." The chief paused as if to find the strength to voice his next words. "We are going to have to leave the old ones behind."

His eyes quickly scanned the crowd for reactions. But the hunger and cold had taken their toll, and The People did not seem to be shocked. Many expected this to happen, and some thought it for the best. In those days, leaving the old behind in times of starvation was not an unknown act, although in this band it was happening for the first time. The starkness of the primitive land seemed to demand it, as the people, to survive, were forced to imitate some of the ways of the animals. Like the younger, more able wolves who shun the old leader of the pack, these people would leave the old behind so that they could move faster without the extra burden.

The older woman, Ch'idzigyaak, had a daughter and a grandson among the group. The chief looked into the crowd for them and saw that they, too, had shown no reaction. Greatly relieved that the unpleasant anouncement had been made without incident, the chief instructed everyone to pack immediately. Meanwhile, this brave man who was their leader could not bring himself to look at the two old women, for he did not feel so strong now.

The chief understood why The People who cared for the old women did not raise objections. In these hard times, many of the men became frustrated and were angered easily, and one wrong thing said or done could cause an uproar and make matters worse. So it was that the weak and beaten members of the tribe kept what dismay they felt to themselves, for they knew that the cold could bring on a wave of panic followed by cruelty and brutality among people fighting for survival.

In the many years the women had been with the band, the chief had come to feel affection for them. Now, he wanted to be away as quickly as possible so that the two old women could not look at him and make him feel worse than he had ever felt in his life.

The two women sat old and small before the

campfire with their chins held up proudly, disguising their shock. In their younger days they had seen very old people left behind, but they never expected such a fate. They stared ahead numbly as if they had not heard the chief condemn them to a certain death — to be left alone to fend for themselves in a land that understood only strength. Two weak old women stood no chance against such a rule. The news left them without words or action and no way to defend themselves.

Of the two, Ch'idzigyaak was the only one with a family — a daughter, Ozhii Nelii, and a grandson, Shruh Zhuu. She waited for her daughter to protest, but none came, and a deeper sense of shock overcame her. Not even her own daughter would try to protect her. Next to her, Sa' also was stunned. Her mind reeled and, though she wanted to cry out, no words came. She felt as if she were in a terrible nightmare where she could neither move nor speak.

As the band slowly trudged away,

Ch'idzigyaak's daughter went over to her mother, carrying a bundle of babiche — thickly stripped raw moosehide that served many purposes. She hung her head in shame and grief, for her mother refused to acknowledge her presence. Instead, Ch'idzigyaak stared unflinchingly ahead.

Ozhii Nelii was in deep turmoil. She feared that if she defended her mother, The People would settle the matter by leaving her behind and her son, too. Worse yet, in their famished state, they might do something even more terrible. She could not chance it.

With those frightening thoughts, Ozhii Nelii silently begged with sorrowful eyes for forgiveness and understanding as she gently laid the babiche down in front of her rigid parent. Then she slowly turned and walked away with a heaviness in her heart, knowing she had just lost her mother.

The grandson, Shruh Zhuu, was deeply disturbed by the cruelty. He was an unusual boy. While the other boys competed for their manhood by hunting and wrestling, this one was content to help provide for his mother and the two old women. His behavior seemed to be outside of the structure of the band's organization handed down from generation to generation. In this case, the women did most of the burdensome tasks such as pulling the well-packed toboggans. In addition, much other time-consuming work was expected to be done by the women while the men concentrated on hunting so that the band could survive. No one complained, for that was the way things were and always had been.

Shruh Zhuu held much respect for the women. He saw how they were treated and he disapproved. And while it was explained to him over and over, he never understood why the men did not help the women. But his training told him that he never was to question the ways of The People, for that would be disrespectful. When he was younger, Shruh Zhuu was not afraid to voice his opinions on this subject, for youth and innocence were his guardians. Later, he learned that such behavior invited punishment. He felt the pain of the silent treatment when even his mother refused to speak to him for days. So Shruh Zhuu learned that it caused less pain to think about certain things than to speak out about them.

Although he thought abandoning the helpless old women was the worst thing The People could do, Shruh Zhuu was struggling with himself. His mother saw the turmoil raging in his eyes and she knew that he was close to protesting. She went to him quickly and whispered urgently into his ear not to think of it, for the men were desperate enough to commit any kind of cruel action. Shruh Zhuu saw the men's dark faces and knew this to be true, so he held his tongue even as his heart continued to rage rebelliously.

In those days, each young boy was trained to care for his weapons, sometimes better than he cared for his loved ones, for the weapons were to be his livelihood when he became a man. When a boy was caught handling his weapon the wrong way or for the wrong purpose, it resulted in harsh punishment. As he grew older, the boy would learn the power of his weapon and how much significance it had, not only for his own survival but also for that of his people.

Shruh Zhuu threw all this training and thoughts of his own safety to the winds. He took from his belt a hatchet made of sharpened animal bones bound tightly together with hardened babiche and stealthily placed it high in the thick boughs of a bushy young spruce tree, well concealed from the eyes of The People.

As Shruh Zhuu's mother packed their things, he turned toward his grandmother. Though she seemed to look right through him, Shruh Zhuu made sure no one was watching as he pointed to his empty belt, then toward the spruce tree. Once more he gave his grandmother a look of hopelessness, and reluctantly turned and walked away to join the others, wishing with a sinking

feeling that he could do something miraculous
to end this nightmarish day.

The large band of famished people slowly
moved away, leaving the two women sitting in
the same stunned position on their piled spruce
boughs. Their small fire cast a soft orange glow
onto their weathered faces. A long time passed
before the cold brought Ch'idzigyaak out of her
stupor. She was aware of her daughter's helpless

gesture but believed that her only child should have defended her even in the face of danger. The old woman's heart softened as she thought of her grandson. How could she bear hard feelings toward one so young and gentle? The others made her angry, especially her daughter! Had she not trained her to be strong? Hot, unbidden tears ran from her eyes.

At that moment, Sa' lifted her head in time to see her friend's tears. A rush of anger surged within her. How dare they! Her cheeks burned with the humiliation. She and the other old woman were not close to dying! Had they not sewed and tanned for what the people gave them? They did not have to be carried from camp to camp. They were neither helpless nor hopeless. Yet they had been condemned to die.

Her friend had seen eighty summers, she, seventy-five. The old ones she had seen left behind when she was young were so close to death that some were blind and could not walk. Now here she was, still able to walk, to see, to talk, yet… bah! Younger people these days looked for easier ways out of hard times. As the cold air smothered the campfire, Sa' came alive with a greater fire within her, almost as if her spirit had absorbed the energy from the now-glowing embers of the campfire. She went to the tree and retrieved the hatchet, smiling softly as she thought of her friend's grandson. She sighed as she walked toward her companion, who had not stirred.

Sa' looked up at the blue sky. To an experienced eye, the blue this time of winter meant cold. Soon it would be colder yet as night approached. With a worried frown on her face, Sa' kneeled beside her friend and spoke in a gentle but firm voice. "My friend," she said and paused, hoping for more strength than she felt. "We can sit here and wait to die. We will not have long to wait…

"Our time of leaving this world should not come for a long time yet," she added quickly when her friend looked up with panic-stricken eyes. "But we will die if we just sit here and wait. This would prove them right about our helplessness."

Ch'idzigyaak listened with despair. Knowing that her friend was dangerously close to accepting a fate of death from cold and hunger, Sa' spoke more urgently. "Yes, in their own way they have condemned us to die! They think that we are too old and useless. They forget that we, too, have earned the right to live! So I say if we are going to die, my friend, let us die trying, not sitting."

CHAPTER 2
"Let us die trying"

Ch'idzigyaak sat quietly as if trying to make up her confused mind. A small feeling of hope sparked in the blackness of her being as she listened to her friend's strong words. She felt the cold stinging her cheeks where her tears had fallen, and she listened to the silence that The People left behind. She knew that what her friend said was true, that within this calm, cold land waited a certain death if they did nothing for themselves. Finally, more in desperation than in determination she echoed her friend's words: "Let us die trying." With that, her friend helped her up off the sodden branches.

The women gathered sticks to build the fire and they added pieces of fungus that grew large and dry on fallen cottonwood trees to keep it smoldering. They went around to other campfires to salvage what embers they could find. As they packed to travel, the migrating bands in these times preserved hot coals in hardened mooseskin sacks or birchbark containers filled with ash in which the embers pulsated, ready to spark the next campfire.

As night approached, the women cut thin strips from the bundle of babiche, fashioning them into nooses the size of a rabbit's head. Then, despite their weariness, the women managed to make some rabbit snares, which they immediately set out.

The moon hung big and orange on the horizon as they trudged through the knee-deep snow, searching in the dimness for signs of rabbit life. It was hard to see, and what rabbits existed stayed quiet in the cold weather. But they found several old, hardened rabbit trails frozen solid beneath the trees and arching willows. Ch'idzigyaak tied a babiche noose to a long, thick willow branch and placed it across one of the trails. She made little fences of willows and spruce boughs on each side of the noose to guide the rabbit through the snare. The two women set a few more snares but felt little hope that even one rabbit would be caught.

On their way back to the camp, Sa' heard something skitter lightly along the bark of a tree. She stood very still, motioning her friend to do the same. Both women strained to hear the sound once more in the silence of the night. On a tree not far from them, silhouetted in the now-silvery moonlight, they saw an adventurous tree squirrel. Sa' slowly reached to her belt for the hatchet. With her eyes on the squirrel and her movements deliberately slow, she aimed the hatchet toward this target that represented survival. The animal's small head came up instantly and as Sa' moved her hand to throw, the squirrel darted up the tree. Sa' foresaw this, and, aiming a little higher, ended the small animal's life in one calculating throw with skill and hunting knowledge that she had not used in many seasons.

Ch'idzigyaak let out a deep sigh of relief. The moon's light shone on the younger woman's smiling face as she said in a proud yet shaky voice, "Many times I have done that, but never did I think I would do it again."

Back at the camp, the women boiled the squirrel meat in snow water and drank the broth, saving the small portion of meat to be eaten later, for they knew that otherwise, this could be their last meal.

The two women had not eaten for some time because The People had tried to conserve what little food they had. Now they realized why precious food had not been given to them. Why waste food on two who were to die? Trying not to think about what had happened, the two women filled their empty stomachs with the warm squirrel broth and settled down in their tents for the night.

The shelter was made of two large caribou hides wrapped around three long sticks shaped into a kind of triangle. Inside were thickly piled spruce boughs covered with many fur blankets. The women were aware that, although they had been left behind to fend for themselves, The

People had done them a good deed by leaving them with all their possessions. They suspected that the chief was responsible for this small kindness. Other less noble members of the band would have decided that the two women soon would die and would have pilfered everything except for the warm fur and skin clothing they wore. With these confusing thoughts lingering in their minds, the two frail women dozed.

The moonlight shone silently upon the frozen earth as life whispered throughout the land, broken now and then by a lone wolf's melancholy howl. The women's eyes twitched in tired, troubled dreams, and soft helpless moans escaped from their lips. Then a cry rang out somewhere in the night as the moon dipped low on the western horizon. Both women awoke at once, hoping that the awful screech was a part of her nightmare. Again the wail was heard. This time, the women recognized it as the sound of something caught in one of their snares. They were relieved. Fearing that other predators would beat them to their catch, the women hurriedly dressed and rushed to their snare sets. There they saw a small, trembling rabbit that lay partially strangled as it eyed them warily. Without hesitation, Sa' went to the rabbit, put one hand around its neck, felt for the beating heart, and squeezed until the small struggling animal went limp. After Sa' reset the snare, they went back to the camp, each feeling a thread of new hope.

Morning came, but brought no light to this far northern land. Ch'idzigyaak awoke first. She slowly kindled the fire into a flame as she carefully added more wood. When the fire had died out during the cold night, frost from their warm breathing had accumulated on the walls of caribou skins.

Sighing in dull exasperation, Ch'idzigyaak went outside where the northern lights still danced above and the stars winked in great numbers. Ch'idzigyaak stood for a moment staring up at these wonders. In all her years, the night sky never failed to fill her with awe.

Remembering her task, Ch'idzigyaak grabbed the upper rims of the caribou skins, laid them on the ground and briskly brushed off the crystal frost. After putting the skins up again, she went back inside to build up the campfire. Soon moisture dripped from the skin wall, which quickly dried.

Ch'idzigyaak shuddered to think of the melting frost dripping on them in the cold weather. How had they managed before? Ah, yes! The younger ones were always there, piling wood on the fire, peering into the shelter to make sure that their elders' fire did not go out. What a pampered pair they had been! How would they survive now?

Ch'idzigyaak sighed deeply, trying not to dwell on those dark thoughts, and concentrated instead on tending the fire without waking her sleeping companion. The shelter warmed as the fire crackled, spitting tiny sparks from the dry wood. Slowly, Sa' awoke to this sound and lay on her back for a long time before becoming aware of her friend's movement. Turning her aching neck slowly she began to smile but stopped as she saw her friend's forlorn look. In a pained grimace Sa' propped herself up carefully on one elbow and tried to smile encouragingly as she said, "I thought yesterday had only been a dream when I awoke to your warm fire."

Ch'idzigyaak managed a slight smile at the obvious attempt to lift her spirits but continued to stare dully into the fire. "I sit and worry," she said after a long silence. "I fear what lies ahead. No! Don't say anything!" She held up her hands as her friend opened her mouth to speak.

"I know that you are sure of our survival. You are younger." She could not help but smile bitterly at her remark, for just yesterday they both had been judged too old to live with the young. "It has been a long time since I have been on my own. There has always been someone there to take care of me, and now…" She broke off with a hoarse whisper as tears fell, much to her shame.

Her friend let her cry. As the tears eased and

the older woman wiped her dampened face, she laughed. "Forgive me, my friend. I am older than you. Yet I cry like a baby."

"We are like babies," Sa' responded. The older woman looked up in surprise at such an admission. "We are like helpless babies." A smile twitched her lips as her friend started to look slightly affronted by the remark, but before Ch'idzigyaak could take it in the wrong way Sa' went on. "We have learned much during our long lives. Yet there we were in our old age, thinking that we had done our share in life. So we stopped, just like that. No more working like we used to, even though our bodies are still healthy enough to do a little more than we expect of ourselves."

Ch'idzigyaak sat listening, alert to her friend's sudden revelation as to why the younger ones thought it best to leave them behind. "Two old women. They complain, never satisfied. We talk of no food, and of how good it was in our days when it really was no better. We think that we are so old. Now, because we have spent so many years convincing the younger people that we are helpless, they believe that we are no longer of use to this world."

Seeing tears fill her friend's eyes at the finality of her words, Sa' continued in a voice heavy with feeling. "We are going to prove them wrong! The People. And death!" She shook her head, motioning into the air. "Yes, it awaits us, this death. Ready to grab us the moment we show our weak spots. I fear this kind of death more than any suffering you and I will go through. If we are going to die anyway, let us die trying!"

Ch'idzigyaak stared for a long time at her friend and knew that what she said was true, that death surely would come if they did not try to survive. She was not convinced that the two of them were strong enough to make it through the harsh season, but the passion in her friend's voice made her feel a little better. So, instead of feeling sadness because there was nothing further they could say or do, she smiled. "I think we said this before and will probably say it many more times, but yes, let us die trying." And with a sense of strength filling her like she had not thought possible, Sa' returned the smile as she got up to prepare for the long day ahead of them.

CHAPTER 3
Recalling old skills

*T*hat day the women went back in time to recall the skills and knowledge that they had been taught from early childhood.

They began by making snowshoes. Usually birchwood was collected during late spring and early summer, but today the young birch would have to do. They didn't have the correct tools, of course, but the women managed with what they had to split the wood into four parts each, which they boiled in their large birch containers. When the wood became soft, the women bent it roundish and pointed at the tips. Putting two of these half-rounded sides together, the women awkwardly drilled many little holes into both sides with their small pointed sewing awls. The work was hard, but despite their aching fingers the women continued until they finished the task. Earlier, they had soaked the babiche in water. Now they took the softened material, sliced it into thin strips, and wove it onto the snowshoes. As the babiche hardened with a little help from the campfire, the women prepared leather bindings for their snowshoes.

When they finished, the women beamed with pride. Then they walked atop the snow with their slightly awkward but serviceable snowshoes to check their rabbit snares and were further cheered to find they had caught another rabbit. The knowledge that a few days before The People had tried to snare rabbits in the area without success made the women feel almost superstitious about their good luck. They went back to the camp feeling lighthearted about all that had been accomplished.

That night the women talked about their plans. They agreed that they could not remain in the fall camp where they had been abandoned, for there were not enough animals on which to survive the long winter. They also were afraid that potential enemies might come upon them. Other bands were traveling, too, even in the cold winter, and the women did not want to be exposed to such dangers. They also began to fear their own people because of the broken trust. The two women decided they must move on, fearing that the cold weather would force people to do desperate things to survive, remembering the taboo stories handed down for generations about how some had turned into cannibals to survive.

The two women sat in the shelter, thinking about where to go. Suddenly Ch'idzigyaak burst out, "I know of a place!"

"Where?" Sa' asked in an excited voice.

"Do you remember the place where we fished long ago? The creek where the fish were so abundant that we had to build many caches to dry them?" The younger woman searched her memory for a moment, and vaguely the place came to mind. "Yes, I do remember. But why did we not ever return?" she asked. Ch'idzigyaak shrugged. She did not know either.

"Maybe The People forgot that place existed," she ventured.

Whatever the reason, the two women agreed

that it would be a good place to go now and since it was a long distance, they should leave at once. The women yearned to be as far away as possible from this place of bad memories.

The following morning they packed. Their caribou skins served many purposes. That day, they served as pulling sleds. Taking the two skins off the tent frame, the women laid the skins flat with the fur facing the snow. They packed their possessions neatly in the skins and laced them tightly shut with long strips of babiche. They fastened long woven ropes of mooseskin leather onto the front of the skin sleds, and each woman tied a rope around her waist. With the fur of the caribou hides sliding lightly across the dry, deep snow and the women's snowshoes making the walking easier, the two women began their long journey.

Temperatures had dropped, and the cold air made the women's eyes sting. Time and time again, they had to warm their faces with their bare hands, and they continually wiped tears from their irritated eyes. But their fur and skin clothing served them well, for cold as it was, their bodies remained warm.

The women walked late into the night. They had not gone too far, but both were bone-weary and felt as though they had been walking forever. Deciding to camp, the women dug deep pits in the snow and filled them with spruce boughs. Then they built a small campfire, reboiling the squirrel meat and drinking its broth. They were so tired they soon fell asleep. This time they did not moan or twitch but slept deeply and soundlessly.

Morning arrived, and the women awoke to the deep cold surrounding them while the sky above seemed like a bowl of stars. But as the women tried to climb out of their pits, their bodies would not move. Looking into each other's eyes, the women realized they had pushed their bodies beyond their physical endurance. Finally, the younger, more determined Sa' managed to move. But the pain was so great that she let out an agonized groan. Knowing this would happen to her, too, Ch'idzigyaak lay still for awhile, gathering courage to withstand the pain she knew would come. Finally, she, too, made her way slowly and painfully out of the snow shelter, and the women limped around the camp to loosen their stiff joints. After they chewed on the remaining squirrel meat, they continued their journey, slowly pulling their laden toboggans.

That day would be remembered as one of the longest and hardest of the days to come. They stumbled numbly on, many times falling down into the snow from sheer fatigue and old age. Yet they pushed on, almost in desperation, knowing that each step brought them nearer to their destination.

The distant sunlight that appeared for a short while each day peeped hazily through the ice fog that hung in the air. Now and again, blue skies could be seen, but mostly the women noticed only their own frosty breath coming in thick swirls. Freezing their lungs was another worry, and they took care not to work too hard in the cold and, if such work was unavoidable, they wore a protective covering over their faces. This could cause irritating side effects, such as frost buildup where the covering brushed against their faces. However, the women did not notice such minor discomforts compared with their aching limbs, stiff joints, and swollen feet. Sometimes even the heavy sleds seemed to serve a purpose by keeping the women from falling flat on their faces as they pulled onward with the ropes wrapped around their chests.

As the few hours of daylight slipped away, the women's eyes readjusted to the darkness that began to enfold them. But they knew that night had not yet arrived and that there was still time to move. When it became time to camp, the women found themselves on a large lake. They could see the outline of trees along the shore and they knew that the forest would be a better place to camp. But they were so exhausted they could go no farther. Again they dug a deep pit in the snow, and after snuggling down and covering themselves with their skin blankets they were soon asleep. The thick skin and fur clothing held their body heat and protected them from the cold air. The snow pit was as warm as any shelter aboveground, so the women slept, mindless of freezing temperatures that made even the most ferocious northern animals seek shelter.

The next morning, Sa' awoke first. The long sleep and cold air cleared her mind considerably. With a twisting grimace she stuck her head out of the hole to look around. She saw the outline of trees on the shore and remembered how they had been too tired to complete their crossing of the lake.

She got up slowly, not wanting to disturb her friend's slumber and knowing that with a wrong move her stiffened body would lock up and refuse to go farther. A smile hovered around her lips as she thought of how she and her friend had complained loudly and often of their minor aches and pains a few days before, and of the walking sticks they had used until forgetting them at the camp the day before. Slowly stretching in the chilly air, she made a mental note to remind her friend of this when the right time came. They could laugh over the fact that for years they had carried those sticks around to help them walk better and now, somehow, they had managed many miles without them. Putting on her snowshoes, Sa' walked about to loosen the stiffness in her sore joints.

From within the snow pit, Ch'idzigyaak looked up at her more agile companion who slowly circled the shelter. Ch'idzigyaak was still tired and feeling miserable. But she knew she must do her best to stand beside her friend through this hardship. She had lived long enough to know that if she gave up, her friend would give up, too. So she forced herself to move, but the pain that filled her body made her lie back down, and let out a deep sigh.

Sa' saw that Ch'idzigyaak was having a hard time, so she reached down to help her climb out of the pit. Together they grunted, struggling to move. Soon they were walking again, and kept right on going until they reached the edge of the lake. There, they built a fire and, after eating some of the rabbit meat they had carefully rationed, they returned for their sleds and resumed their journey.

The frozen lakes seemed endless. Struggling through the many spruce trees, willow thickets, and thorn patches that lay between the lakes wore the women out until they felt as if they had traveled many more miles than they had. Despite having to make many detours around obstacles, the women never completely lost their sense of direction. Sometimes, fatigue clouded their judgement, and they found themselves straying slightly off course or going in circles, but they soon found their way again. In vain, they hoped that the slough they sought would appear suddenly. Indeed, there were times when one of them would fantasize that they had reached their destination. But the constant reminders of the intense cold and aching bones brought them quickly back to reality.

On the fourth night, the women almost stumbled onto the slough. Everything around them stood shrouded under silvery moonlight. Shadows stretched beneath the many trees and over the slough. The women stood on the bank for a few moments, resting as their eyes took in the beauty of that special night. Sa' marveled at the power the land held over people like herself, over the animals, and even over the trees. They all depended on the land, and if its rules were not obeyed, quick and nonjudgmental death could fall upon the careless and unworthy. Ch'idzigyaak looked at her friend as Sa' sighed deeply. "What's the matter?" she asked.

Sa's face creased in a sad smile. "Nothing is wrong, my friend. We are on the right trail after all. I was thinking about how it used to be that the land was easy for me to live on, and now it seems not to want me. Perhaps it is just my aching joints that are making me complain."

Ch'idzigyaak laughed. "Perhaps it is because our bodies are just too old, or maybe we are out of shape. Maybe the time will come when we will spring across this land again." Sa' joined in the joke.

Such musings were meant only to lift their spirits and the women knew that their journey was not over, nor would their struggle for survival become easier. Although they had grown soft in their old age, Ch'idzigyaak and Sa' knew they would pay a high price of hard toil before the land yielded them any comforts.

The two women walked down the winding slough until they came upon a large river. Even in times of cold weather, the swishing undercurrents of the river eroded the ice and made it thin and dangerous to walk on. The women realized this as they carefully inched their way across the quiet river, keeping their senses alert for the sound of cracking ice or any hint of steam rising from between the ice chinks.

When they finally reached the other side, the tension and fatigue left both women mentally and physically drained. With what little energy remained, they numbly set to the task of building yet another overnight shelter.

Chapter 4
A painful journey

Nights past when they had managed to build shelters were nothing compared to this one, for the women were so tired they could barely move. In blind determination they stumbled about gathering spruce boughs for their beds and large chunks of wood for the campfire. Finally, they huddled together and stared as if hypnotized into the large orange blaze they ignited from the live coals carried from the first campsite. Soon they slipped mind-lessly off to sleep. They did not hear the lonesome howl of a distant wolf, and before they knew it the cold air of morning brought them back to their senses.

They had fallen asleep leaning against one another and somehow managed to stay in that position all night. Because they were sitting up on their legs, the women knew getting up would not be easy. They sat still for a long time. Then Sa' made an effort to rise, but her legs had lost their feeling. She grunted and tried again. Mean-while, Ch'idzigyaak closed her eyes tightly and pretended to be asleep. She did not want to face the day.

Sa' gathered a little courage to force herself to move, but the aches in her bones proved to be too much for her this time. Again they had pushed their bodies beyond their limits. With-out meaning to, Sa' let out a painful moan, and she felt a great urge to cry. She hung her head, defeated by all they had been through these past few days, and the cold made her feel even more despair. As much as she wanted to, her body would not move. She was too stiff.

Ch'idzigyaak listened lethargically to her friend's sniffles. She was amazed that she could sit and listen to Sa' cry and feel no emotion. Perhaps it was not meant for them to go on. Perhaps the young ones were right — she and Sa' were fighting the inevitable. It would be easy for them to snuggle deeper into the warmth of their fur clothing and fall asleep. They would not have to prove anything to anyone anymore. Perhaps the sleep that Sa' feared would not be so bad after all. At least, Ch'idzigyaak thought to herself, it would not be as bad as this.

Yet, for as little will as her older friend had, Sa' possessed enough determination for both of them. Shrugging off the cold, the pain in her sides, her empty stomach, and the numbness in her legs, she struggled to get up and this time succeeded. As had become her morning habit, she limped around the campsite until feeling slowly began to course through her bloodstream. When the circulation returned, there was more pain. But Sa' concentrated her attention on gathering more wood to build the fire. Then she boiled a rabbit head to make a tasty broth.

Ch'idzigyaak watched all this from between narrowed lids. She did not want her friend to know that she was awake, for then, Ch'idzigyaak felt, she would be obligated to move, and she did not want to move. Not now and not ever. She would stay exactly as she was, and perhaps death would steal her quickly away from the suffering. But her body was not ready to give in just yet. Instead of slipping blissfully into oblivion, Ch'idzigyaak suddenly felt the urgent need to relieve her bladder. She tried to ignore this, but soon her bladder could wait no more, and with a loud grunt she felt her bladder letting go. In quick panic she jumped up and headed for the willows, startling her friend. When Ch'idzigyaak came out of the willows looking slightly guilty, Sa' tilted her head in wonder. "Is something wrong?" she asked. Ch'idzigyaak, feeling embarrassed, admitted, "I surprised myself by how fast I moved. I did not think I would be able to move at all!"

Sa' was thinking of the day ahead. "After we have eaten, we should try to move on, even if we go only a little way today," she said. "Each step brings us closer to where we are going. Although I do not feel good today, my mind has power over my body, and it wants us to move on instead of staying here to rest — which is what I want to do." Ch'idzigyaak listened as she ate her portion of the rabbit head and broth. She, too, felt like staying there for a while. In fact, she desperately wanted to stay. But after putting aside her foolish thoughts, she felt ashamed and reluctantly agreed they should move on.

Sa' felt a slight disappointment when Ch'idzigyaak agreed to resume their journey, wondering if deep within her she had hoped Ch'idzigyaak would refuse to move. But it was too late for second thoughts. So both women tied the ropes around their thin waists and pulled onward. As they walked, they kept their eyes open for signs of animals, for their food was nearly gone, and meat was their prime source of energy. Without it, their struggle would be over soon. Sometimes, the women stopped to discuss the route they had chosen and to ask themselves if it was the correct way. But the river led in only one direction from the slough, so the women walked along the riverbank as they kept a lookout for the narrow creek that would lead them to a place remembered for its plentiful fish long ago.

The days dragged on as the women slowly pulled their sleds across the deep snow. On the sixth day, Sa', who had grown accustomed to staring dully only at the path ahead, happened to glance up. Across the river she saw the opening to the creek. "We are there," she said in a soft, breathless voice. Ch'idzigyaak looked at her friend, then at the creek. "Except we are on the wrong side," she said. Sa' had to smile at her friend, who always seemed to find the negative side of a situation. Too tired to offer a lighter point of view, Sa' sighed to herself as she motioned to her friend to follow.

This time the two women did not worry about hidden cracks beneath the ice. They were too tired. Mindless of the danger, they crossed the frozen river and kept right on going up the tributary. The women walked until late that night. The moon slowly emerged over the trees until it hovered above them, lighting their way along the narrow creek. Although they had walked more hours than they had on earlier days, the women continued on. They felt sure the old campsite was near and they wanted to reach their destination that night.

Just about the time Ch'idzigyaak was ready to beg her friend to stop, she saw the campsite. "Look over there!" she cried. "There are the fishracks we hung so long ago!" Sa' stopped and suddenly felt weak. It was with great effort that she stood on her shaking legs, for a feeling of somehow coming home suddenly over-whelmed her.

Ch'idzigyaak moved closer to her friend and gently placed an arm around her. They looked at each other and felt a surge of powerful emotion that left them speechless. They had traveled all this way by themselves. Good memories came back to them about the place where they had shared much happiness with friends and family. Now, because of an ugly twist of fate, they were here alone, betrayed by those same people. Be-cause they were thrown together in hardship, the two women developed a sense of knowing what the other was thinking, and Sa' was usually the more sensitive one.

"It is better not to think of why we are here," she said. "We must set up our camp here tonight. Tomorrow we will talk." Clearing the bitter emo-tion from her throat, Ch'idzigyaak heartily agreed. So, with slow, dragging movements, the two women climbed up the low bank of the creek and walked to the campsite, where they found an old

tent frame that they used for shelter that night.

Though their clothing shielded them from the awful cold, the caribou skins did a better job. Coals from the fire pulsated amidst the ash all through the night and kept the shelter warm. Finally, the morning cold seeped through, and the women began to stir. Sa' was the first to move. This time her body did not protest so much as she moved about the shelter, placing the wood they had gathered the night before on the tiny embers still burning in the fireplace. After a few moments of softly blowing the dried sticks, a flame began a gentle dance as it spread onto the bundle of dry willows. Soon the shelter was warm and glowing.

That day, the women worked steadily, unmindful of their aching joints. They knew they would have to hurry to make final preparations for the worst of the winter, for even colder weather lay ahead. So they spent the day piling snow high around the shelter to insulate it and gathering all the loose wood they could find. Then without resting, they set a long line of rabbit snares, for the area was rich in willow, and there were many signs of rabbit life. Nighttime had arrived when the women made their way back to the camp. Sa' boiled the remains of the rabbit's innards and the women feasted on the last of their food. After that, they leaned against their bedding and stared into the campfire.

The two women had not known each other well before being abandoned. They had been two neighbors who thrived on each other's bad habit of complaining and on sharing conversations about things that did not matter. Now, their old age and their cruel fate were all they had in common. So it was that night, at the end of their painful journey together, they did not know how to converse in companionship, and instead, each woman dwelled on her own thoughts.

Ch'idzigyaak's mind went immediately to her daughter and grandson. She wondered if they were all right. A surge of hurt streaked through her as she thought about her daughter again. It was still hard for Ch'idzigyaak to believe that her own flesh and blood would refuse to come to her aid. As the self-pity overwhelmed her, Ch'idzigyaak fought the tears that threatened to spill from her eyes, and her lips formed a thin, rigid line. She would not cry! This was the time to be strong and to forget! But with that thought a huge single tear dripped down. She looked at Sa' and saw that she also was lost deep in thought. Ch'idzigyaak was perplexed by her friend. Except for a few moments of weakness, the woman next to her seemed strong and sure of herself, almost as if she were challenged by all of this. Curiosity replaced her pain and Sa' was startled when Ch'idzigyaak spoke.

"Once when I was a little girl, they left my grandmother behind. She could no longer walk and could hardly see. We were so hungry that people were staggering around, and my mother whispered that she was afraid that people would think of eating people. I had not heard of anything like this before, but my family told stories of some who had grown desperate enough to do such things. My heart filled with fear as I clung to my mother's hand. If someone looked into my eyes, I would turn my head quickly, fearing he might take notice of me and consider eating me. That is how much fear I had. I was hungry, too, but somehow it didn't matter. Perhaps it was because I was so young and had my family all around me. When they talked about leaving my grandmother behind, I was horrified. I remember my father and brothers arguing with the rest of the men, but when my father came back to the shelter, I looked at his face and knew what would happen. Then I looked at my grandmother. She was blind and too deaf to hear what was going on." Ch'idzigyaak took a deep breath before continuing with her story.

"When they bundled her up and put her blankets all around her, I think Grandmother sensed what was happening because as we began to leave the camp I could hear her crying." The older woman shuddered at the memory.

"Later, when I grew up, I learned that my brother and father went back to end my grandmother's life, for they did not want her to suffer. And they burned her body in case anyone thought of filling their bellies with her flesh. Somehow, we survived that winter, though my only real memory of that time was that it was not a happy one. I remember other times of empty stomachs, but none as bad as that one winter."

Sa' smiled sadly, understanding her friend's painful memories. She, too, remembered. "When I was young, I was like a boy," she began. "I was always with my brothers. I learned many things from them. Sometimes, my mother would try to make me sit still and sew, or learn that which I would have to know when I became a woman. But my father and brothers always rescued me. They liked me the way I was." She smiled at her memories.

"Our family was different from most. My father and mother let us do almost anything. We did chores like everyone else, but after they were done, we could explore. I never played with other children, only with my brothers. I am afraid I did not know what growing up was about because I was having so much fun. When my mother asked me if I had become a woman yet, I did not understand. I thought she meant in age, not in that way. And summer after summer, she would ask me the same question, and each time she looked more worried. I did not pay much attention to her. But as I grew as tall as my mother and just a little shorter than my brothers, people looked at me in a strange way. Girls younger than me already were with child and man. Yet I was still free like a child." Sa' laughed heartily as she now knew why she received all those strange looks from people then.

"I began to hear them laugh at me behind my back and I became confused. In a way, I did not care what people thought about me, so I continued to hunt, fish, explore, and do what I pleased. My mother tried to make me stay home and work, but I rebelled. My brothers had taken women, and I told my mother she had plenty of help, and with that I would escape. When my mother turned to my father to discipline me, I would show up with a huge bundle of ducks, fish, or some other food, and my father would say, 'Leave her alone.' Then I grew older, beyond that age when women should have man and child, and everyone was talking about me. I could not understand why, for although I was not with a man and having children, I was still doing my share of the work by providing food. There were times when I brought more food than the men. This did not seem to please them. About this time in my life, we experienced our worst winter. It was cold like this." Sa' motioned with her hand.

"Even babies died, and grown men began to panic, for as hard as they tried they could not find enough animals to eat. There was an old woman in our group whom I rarely noticed. The chief decided we had to move on in our search for food. There was a rumor that far away we would find caribou. This excited everyone.

"The old woman had to be carried. The chief did not want this burden, so he told everyone that we would leave her behind. No one argued, except me. My mother tried to stifle me, but I was young and unthinking. She told me that this was to be done for the sake of the whole group. She seemed like a cold, unfeeling stranger as she tried to talk me out of my protest, but I angrily brushed her off. I was shocked and furious. I felt that The People were being lazy and were not thinking clearly. It was my job to talk some sense into them. And being who I was, I spoke up for the woman whom I hardly knew existed until then. I asked the men if they thought they were no better than the wolves who would shun their old and weak.

"The chief was a cruel man. I had avoided him until the day I stood before him and shouted angry words at his face. I could see that he was twice as angry as I was, but I could not stop myself. Even though I knew that the chief disliked me, I argued on, not listening to him as he tried to answer my accusations. His action was wrong, and I meant to make it right. As I continued to talk, I was unaware of the shock that awakened the group from its malnourished lethargy. A fearful look fell upon the chief's face and he put his large hand over my mouth. 'All right, strange young girl,' he said in a loud voice that I knew was meant to humiliate me. I could feel my chin go up farther so that he could see that I remained proud and unafraid. 'You will stay with the old one,' he said. I could hear my mother gasp, and my own heart sank. Yet I would not yield as I stared unblinkingly into his eyes.

"My family was deeply hurt, but pride and shame kept them from protesting. They did not want a daughter who would take such a stand against the strong leaders of the group. I did not think the leaders were strong. The chief acted as if I did not exist after that, and I was ignored by everyone else except my family, who begged me to apologize to the leader. But I would not give in. My pride grew with each moment the others pretended I was not there, and I continued to plead for the old woman's life." Sa' broke into laughter at her impetuous youth.

"What happened after that?" Ch'idzigyaak wanted to know.

Sa' paused as she deeply inhaled the pain from those long-ago memories. Continuing in a subdued voice, she said, "After they left, I was not so brave. There were no animals to be found for miles around. But I was determined to show what could be done by my good intentions. So the old woman — I never did know her name, for I was too busy trying to keep us alive — and I ate mice, owls, and anything else that moved. I killed it, and we ate it. The woman died that winter. Then I was alone. Not even my pride and usual carefree ways could help me. I talked to myself all the time. Who else was there? They would think I was crazy if The People returned to find me talking to the air. At least you and I have each other," Sa' told her friend, who nodded in wholehearted agreement.

"Then I realized the importance of being with a large group. The body needs food, but the mind needs people. When the sun finally came hot and long on the land, I explored the country. One day as I was walking along, talking to myself as usual, someone said, 'Who are you talking to?' For a moment I thought I was hearing things. I stopped in my tracks and turned slowly to find a big, strong-looking man with his arms crossed, smiling at me in a bold manner. Many feelings ran through me at that moment. I was surprised, embarrassed, and angry all at once. 'You scared me!' I said, trying to cover up my real feelings. Because my cheeks were burning, I knew I did not fool him, for his grin grew deeper. He asked me what I was doing out there alone, and I told him my story. I felt at that moment that I could trust him. He told me that the same thing happened to him. Only he was banished because he was foolish enough to fight over a woman who was meant for another man. We were together a long time before we became a man and woman together. I never saw my family again, and it was years later that we joined the band.

"Then he tried to fight with a bear and died. Foolish man," she added with grudging admiration, as a deep sadness weighed down her face.

It was the first time Ch'idzigyaak saw her friend so sad, and she broke the silence by saying, "You were luckier than I, for when it became apparent that I was not interested in taking a man, I was forced to live with a man much older than me. I hardly knew him. It was years before we had our child. He was older than I am now when he died."

Sa' laughed. "The People would have chosen a man for me too, had I been with them much longer." After a momentary silence, she continued. "Now here we are, truly old. I hear our bones creaking, and we are left behind to fend for ourselves." The women fell into silence as they struggled with their emotions. They lay on their warm beds as the cold earth trembled outside. They thought about the experiences they had shared. As they fell into an exhausted sleep, each woman felt more at home because of her new knowledge of the other and because each had survived hard times before.

Days shortened as the sun sank deeper under the horizon. It grew so cold there were times when the women jumped as the trees around them cracked loudly from the cold pressure. Even the willows snapped. But as the women settled down they also became depressed. They feared the savage wolves that howled in the distance. Other imagined fears tormented them as well, for there was plenty of time to think as the dark days drifted slowly by. In what daylight they had, the two women forced themselves to move. They spent all their waking hours collecting firewood from underneath the deep snow. Though food was scarce, warmth was their main concern, and at night they would sit and talk, trying to keep each other from the loneliness and fears that threatened to overcome them. The People rarely spent precious time in idle conversation. When they did speak, it was to communicate rather than to socialize. But these women made an exception during the long evenings. They talked. And a sense of mutual respect developed as each learned of the other's past hardships.

Many days went by before the women caught more rabbits. It had been some time since they had eaten a full meal. They managed to preserve their energy by boiling spruce boughs to serve as a minty tea, but it made the stomach sour. Knowing it was dangerous to eat anything solid after such a diet, the two women first boiled the rabbit meat to make a nourishing broth, which they drank slowly. After a day of drinking the broth, the women cautiously ate one ham off a rabbit. As the days passed, they allowed themselves more portions, and soon their energy was restored.

With wood piled high around the shelter like a barricade, the women found that they had more time to forage for food. The hunting skills they learned in their youth reemerged, and each day the women would walk farther from the shelter to set their rabbit snares and to keep an eye out for any other animals small enough to kill. One of the rules they had been taught was that if you set snares for animals you must check them regularly. Neglecting your snareline brought bad luck. So, despite the cold and their own physical discomforts, the two women checked their snares each day and usually found a rabbit to reward them.

At nightfall, when their daily chores were completed, the women wove the rabbit fur into blankets and clothing, such as mittens and face coverings. Sometimes, to break the monotony, one would present a woven rabbit-fur hat or mittens to the other. This always brought wide smiles.

As the days slowly passed, the weather lost

its cold edge, and the women savored moments of glee — they had survived the winter! They regained what energy they had lost and now they kept busy collecting more firewood, checking the rabbit snares and scouting the vast area for other animals. Though the women had lost the habit of complaining, they grew tired of the daily fare of rabbit meat and found themselves dreaming of other game to eat, such as willow grouse, tree squirrels, and beaver meat.

One morning, as Ch'idzigyaak awoke, she felt something was not quite right. Her heart pumped rapidly as she slowly got up, fearing the worst, and peeked out of the shelter. At first, all seemed still. Then suddenly she spotted a flock of willow grouse pecking at some tree debris that had fallen not far away. With trembling hands, she quietly got a long, thin strand of babiche out of her sewing bag and slowly crept out of the tent. Selecting a long stick from the nearby woodpile, she fashioned a noose at the end and began to crawl toward the flock.

Nervously, the birds started to cluck as they became aware of the woman's presence. Knowing that the birds were about to take flight, Ch'idzigyaak stopped for a few minutes to give them time to calm down. They were not too far from her now, and she hoped that Sa' would not awake and make a noise that would scare away the birds. With knees aching and hands slightly trembling, Ch'idzigyaak slowly pushed the stick forward. Some grouse excitedly flew away to another patch of willows nearby, but she steadfastly ignored them as she continued to lift the stick slowly while the remaining birds walked about faster. Ch'idzigyaak concentrated on the grouse closest to her. It made small movements toward the noose, its head nodding back to front. As the birds started noisily to run and fly off, Ch'idzigyaak shoved the noose forward until the bird's head slipped right into it. Then she jerked the stick upward as the bird squawked and twisted until it hung motionless. Standing up with the dead grouse in her hand, Ch'idzigyaak turned toward the tent to find her friend's face wreathed in smiles. Ch'idzigyaak smiled back.

Looking into the air, Ch'idzigyaak took note of a warmth in the air. "The weather gets better," Sa' said softly and the older woman's eyes widened in surprise. "I should have noticed. Had it been cold, I would have frozen in my position of a sneaky fox." The women found great laughter in this as they went back into the shelter to prepare the meat of a different season to come. After that morning, the weather fluctuated between bitter cold and then warm and snowy days. That the women did not catch another bird failed to dampen their spirits, for the days gradually grew longer, warmer, and brighter.

The routes on this map were taken from a regular map of the Yukon Flats area, with the help of my mother. The winter trails are not historically accurate in detail but do show the general areas through which the Gwich'in people traveled for many years before the coming of the Western culture.

Many winter and summer paths were used by the Gwich'in people but through the years, these trails either have been forgotten or changed by younger generations seeking short-cuts, or by natural events.

Ts'it Han (Porcupine River)

Nahtryaa Van

Tr'aanjik

Ditsik ehdlii ddhah

Chahalie Van

Kiahdaii

Njuu Tsal Van

Tsuk Van

J.L.Grant ©93

Trahkyaa Zhraih Van

Chtaatritt Van

Njuu Choh Van

Tokoei Van

Ohtig Van

ARCTIC CIRCLE

Tachyaa Kat (Grass River)

Vunlau Van

CHAPTER 5
Saving a cache of fish

*S*oon *winter was gone and the two old women spent more time hunting game. They feasted on the feisty little squirrels that bolted from tree to tree and on the flocks of willow grouse that seemed to be everywhere.*

With the warm days of spring came the time for muskrat hunting. The women long ago had been tutored in the skills and patience required. First, special nets and traps had to be made. A willow branch was bent into a circle and bound securely at the ends. The women wove thin strips of moose leather into the frames until each formed a crude but sturdy net. Then, on a sunny day, they set out in search of a muskrat tunnel.

They walked a long way before they came to a cluster of lakes with signs of muskrat life. They picked out a lake with little black lumps of muskrat houses still showing on the rotting ice. After locating the muskrat tunnel, the women marked each end of the underground pathway with a stick. When the stick moved, it meant a muskrat was coming through the tunnel and when it emerged from the opening, one of the women would snatch it with her net and end its life with a blow to the head. The first day, the women caught ten muskrats. But they were worn out by the stress of bending down and waiting, so the walk back to camp seemed long.

The spring days brought little time to talk or to reflect on the past as the women kept busy catching more muskrats and some beavers, all of which were smoke-dried for preservation. Their days were so full they hardly took time to eat, and at night they slept deeply. When they decided they had caught more than their share of muskrat and beaver, they packed everything and hauled it back to their main camp.

Still, the women felt vulnerable. The area was rich in animal life now, and they felt in time other people might come. Normally, other people meant their own kind. But since being left behind on that cold winter day, the women felt defenseless against the younger generation and had lost trust that they knew they never could regain. Now, suspicion left them wary of what might happen if anyone were to come upon them and find their growing store of food. They talked about what they should do, and in time they agreed they should move to a place less desirable — a place other people would not wish to explore, perhaps a place where it would be hard to manage the mighty swarms of summer insects.

The women did not relish having to face the many blood-thirsty mosquitoes that awaited them in the thick willow bushes and trees. But their fear of people was greater. So they packed all they had and began the unpleasant trek to the hiding place. They decided to work in the heat of the day when mosquitoes seemed to hide. At night, they sat near a smoky fire to protect themselves. It took days to transfer the camp, but at last, the women stood by the creek and took one last look around, wishing a wind would blow away any hints of their presence.

Before deciding to move, the women had torn large amounts of birch bark from the trees. Now they recognized their mistake. Although by habit they took pieces of bark from trees spaced far apart, the women knew that any alert eye would take notice of this detail. But they also knew that nothing could be done about it, and in resignation they left the camp for their less desirable place within the thickets.

The two women spent the remaining days of spring trying to make their new camp more hospitable. They put up their shelters under the deep shade of tall spruce trees and hidden among many willows. Then they found a cool spot where they dug a deep hole that they lined with willows. There, they laid their large cache of dried meat for the summer. They also placed a few traps atop the ground to scare off any sharp-nosed predators. The mosquitoes were everywhere, and as they worked, the women relied on long-used methods of shielding themselves to keep from being eaten alive. They hung leather tassles around their faces and their thick clothing to keep the small insects from biting into their skin. When it seemed as if they would be carried away, the women covered their skin with muskrat grease to repel the masses of flying pests. Meanwhile, they charted a small hidden path to the creek where they got their water and, with summer nearly upon them, made their fish traps. Once the traps were set, the women had no trouble catching fish and found they had to move nearer to the creek to keep up with the task of cutting and drying. In time, a bear began helping himself to the fish the women had stored. This worried them, but in time they reached an unusual agreement with the bear. They carried the fish guts far from the camp where the greedy bear could laze about and eat at his leisure.

Too soon, the sun lay orange and cool on the evening horizon, and the women knew summer was dwindling. About this time, the spawning salmon began to find their way up the little creek, much to the women's pleasure, and for a short while they were busy with the reddish fish meat. The bear disappeared from the area, but still the women disposed of fish innards far down the creek. If the bear did not eat them, the ever-present ravens would devour them soon enough. The women also were frugal, and they preserved many inside parts of the fish for other uses. For instance, the salmon intestines could be used for containing water, and the skin was fashioned into round bags to hold dried fish. These tasks kept them so busy they were up from early morning until late at night, and before they knew it, the short Arctic summer passed, and fall crept upon them.

When the season changed, the women retired from fishing and hauled their large supply back to the hidden camp. There they found a new problem. They had collected so much fish that there was no place to store it, and with the approaching winter there was no shortage of small animals searching for winter food. Eventually, the women made standing caches for their fish, and they placed great bundles of thorns and brush beneath them to discourage animals from bothering the fish. Perhaps this method worked, or perhaps it was just their luck, but animals kept away from their caches.

Far behind the camp was a low hill that the women had not had time to explore. One day, with their summer hunting finished, Sa' found herself wondering what bounties might lie on that hill or around it. So she took her spear and bow and the arrows the women had made, announcing that she would visit the hill. Ch'idzigyaak did not approve but could see that her friend would not be deterred.

"Just keep the fire going, and your spear nearby, and you should be safe," Sa' said as she set out, leaving Ch'idzigyaak behind shaking her head in disapproval.

It was a day of abandon for Sa'. She felt light-hearted for the first time in more years than she could remember, and like a child, she grasped greedily at the feeling. The day was beautiful. The leaves were turning a brilliant gold and the air was crisp and clear as Sa' all but skipped along an animal trail. From a distance, one would not be able to see that Sa' was an older woman, for she looked lithe and energetic. When she reached the top, she gasped in surprise. Before her lay vast patches of cranberries. Sa' dropped to her knees and began to scoop handfuls of the small red fruit, stuffing them into her mouth. As she gorged on this delicious food, a movement in the nearby brush made her freeze instantly.

Slowly, Sa' forced herself to look toward the sound, imagining the worst. She relaxed when she saw that it was only a bull moose. Then she remembered that this time of year a bull moose could be the most fearful animal on four legs. Usually timid, the bull moose in his rutting stage was no longer afraid of man or of anything else that moved or stood in his way.

The moose remained still for a long time as if he were just as surprised and undecided about the small woman who stood before him as she had been about him. As her pulse slowed almost to normal, Sa' imagined the delectable taste of moosemeat during the long winter months ahead. In another moment of unthinking craziness, she reached for an arrow from her pack and placed it in her bow. The moose's ears flipped forward at the movement, then it turned and ran in the opposite direction just as the arrow landed harmlessly on the soft ground.

Pressing her fate, Sa' followed. She could not run as strongly as when she was young, but with something that looked more like a limp than a jog, Sa' was able to pursue the large animal. A moose can outrun a human any time unless, of course, there is too much snow. But on a snowless day like this, the moose sprinted far ahead as Sa', gasping for breath, barely caught a glimpse of his large hind-end disappearing behind the brush. The big bull stopped many times, almost as if he were playing a game with Sa', and just when she almost caught up, he would saunter far ahead once more. Normally, a moose will run as far as he can from any predator. But today, the moose did not feel much like running, nor did he feel threatened, so the old woman was able to keep him in sight. She was stubborn and would not give up, although she knew that she was outmatched. By late afternoon, the moose seemed to grow tired of the game as he watched her from the corner of his dark round eyes, and with one flip of his ear he began to run faster. Only then did Sa' admit to herself that there was no way she could catch it. She stared at the empty brush in defeat. Slowly she turned back, thinking to herself, "If only I were forty years younger, I might have caught him."

It was late that night when Sa' returned to the camp where her friend kept watch by a large campfire. As Sa' sank wearily into a bundle of spruce boughs, Ch'idzigyaak could not help but blurt out, "I think many more years were taken from me while I worried for you." Despite the admonishment in her voice, Ch'idzigyaak was deeply relieved that no harm had come to her friend.

Knowing that she had been foolish, Sa' understood what her friend had been through and she felt ashamed. Ch'idzigyaak handed her a bowl of warm fish meat and Sa' ate slowly. When a little of her strength returned, Sa' told Ch'idzigyaak how she spent the day. Ch'idzigyaak smiled as she envisioned her friend chasing the long-legged bull, but she did not smile too broadly for it was not in her nature to laugh at others. Sa' was grateful for that, and then, remembering the cranberries, told her friend about the great find and they both were cheered.

It took a few days for Sa' to recover from her adventure with the moose, so the two old women sat still and wove birch bark into large round bowls. Then they went back to the hill and gathered as many berries as they could carry. By that time, autumn was upon them and the nights became chillier, reminding the women that there was no time to waste in gathering their winter wood supply.

They piled wood high around their cache and shelter, and when they cleared all the wood from the area around the camp, they walked far back into the forest, packing in more bundles of wood on their backs. This went on until snowflakes fell from the sky, and one day the women awoke to a land shrouded in white. Now that winter was near, the women spent more time inside their shelter by the warm fire. Their days seemed easier now that they were prepared.

Soon the women fell into a daily routine of collecting wood, checking rabbit snares, and melting snow for water. They sat evenings by the campfire, keeping each other company. During the months past, the women were too busy to think about what had happened to them, and if the thought did cross their minds, they blocked it out. But now that they had nothing else to do in the evenings, those unwelcome thoughts kept coming back until soon each woman began to talk less as each stared thoughtfully into the small fire. They felt it was a taboo to think of those who had abandoned them, but now the treacherous thoughts invaded their minds.

The darkness grew longer, and the land became silent and still. It took much concentration for the two women to fill their long days with work. They made many articles of rabbit-fur clothing such as mittens, hats, and face coverings. Yet, despite this, they felt a great loneliness slowly enclose them.

CHAPTER 6
Sadness among The People

*T*he chief stood surveying his surround-
ings with eyes made a little older by deep
sadness. His people were in a desperate state,
their eyes and cheeks sunk low in gaunt faces
and their tattered clothing barely able to keep
out the freezing cold. Many of them were
frostbitten. Luck had gone against them. In
desperation, still searching for game, they had
returned to the place where they aban-

doned the two old women the winter before.

Sadly, the chief remembered how he fought the urge to turn back and save the old ones. But taking them back into the band would have been the worst thing for him to do. Many of the more ambitious younger men would have seen this as an act of weakness. And the way things had been going, The People would have been easily convinced that their leader was not dependable. No, the chief had known that a drastic change in leadership would have proved more damaging than the hunger, for in times when a band is starving, bad politics lead only to further disaster. The chief remembered that moment of terrible weakness when he had almost allowed his emotions to ruin them all.

Now, once more, The People were suffering, and this winter found them on the verge of hopelessness. After turning their backs on the old women, The People traveled many hard miles before coming on a small herd of caribou. The meat sustained them until spring when they began to harvest fish, ducks, muskrats, and beaver. But just when they regained their energy to hunt and dry their food, the summer season ended, and it was time to think of moving toward the place where they would be able to find winter meat. The chief had never known such terrible luck. As they traveled, the fall season came and went, and once more the band found itself nearly out of food. Now the chief looked at The People wearily with a feeling of panic and self-doubt. How long could he hold out before he, too, became lost in the hunger and fatigue that undermined his decisions? The People seemed to have given up trying to survive. They no longer cared to hear his lectures, staring at him with dulled eyes as if he made no sense.

Something else that troubled the chief was his decision to return to the place where they had left the old women. No one argued as he led them here, but the chief knew they were surprised. Now they stood looking around as if they expected something from him, or expected to see the two women. The chief avoided their eyes, not wanting them to know that he was as confused as they were. There was not a single sign that anyone had been left here. Not one bone gave evidence that the old ones had died. Even if an animal had stripped their bones of flesh, surely something would have been left behind to show that humans had died here. But there was nothing, not even the tent that had sheltered the women.

Among The People was a guide named Daagoo. He was an old man, younger than the two old women, but still considered an elder. In his younger days, Daagoo had been a tracker, but the years had dimmed his vision and skills. He observed out loud what none of the others would acknowledge. "Maybe they moved on," he said in a low voice so that only the chief would hear him. But in the silence, many heard him and some felt a surge of hope for the women many had loved.

After setting up camp, the chief summoned

the guide and three of his strongest young hunters. "I do not know what is going on, but I have a
feeling that all is not as it appears to be. I want
you to go to the camps near here and see what
you can find."

The chief was quiet about what he suspected, but he knew that the guide and the three
hunters would understand, especially Daagoo,
for he had watched the chief from season to
season and had come to know what the man was
thinking. Daagoo respected the chief and realized that he suffered from self-loathing because
of the part he had played in abandoning the old
women. The guide knew the chief despised his
own weakness, for it showed in the hard lines of
bitterness etched on his face. The old man sighed.
He knew that soon the self-hate would take its
toll, and he did not like the thought of a good
man such as the chief being destroyed this way.
Yes, he would try to find out what had happened
to the women, even if the effort was wasted.

Long after the four men left camp the chief

stared after them. He could not find a definite reason why he wasted precious energy and time on what might be a futile effort. Yet he, too, had a strange feeling of hope. Hope for what? He had no answer. All the chief knew for sure was that in hard times The People should hold together, and last winter they had not done so. They had inflicted an injustice on themselves and the two old women, and he knew that The People had suffered silently since that day. It would be good if the two women survived, but the chief knew the odds weighed against that hope. How could two feeble ones survive freezing cold without food or the strength to hunt? The chief acknowledged this, yet he could not still the small speck of hope that sprang from months of hardship. Finding the women alive would give The People a second chance and that, perhaps, was what he hoped for most.

Each of the four men was conditioned to run long distances. What took the two women days to travel to the first camp the year before took the four men a single day. They found nothing but endless snow and trees. The trek taxed their limited energy, and they decided to spend the night there. When the first hint of morning dawned, the men were up and jogging once more.

Daylight was fading when the men arrived at the second camp, and the younger men saw no evidence that it had been used in a long time. Impatience began to overtake them. They had been trained from childhood to respect their elders, but sometimes they thought they knew more than the older ones. Although they did not say so out loud, they felt precious time was being wasted when they should be hunting for moose.

"Let's turn back now," one of the young men suggested, and the others agreed quickly.

The guide's eyes lit up in amusement. How impatient they were! Yet Daagoo did not criticize the others for he, too, had been impatient as a young man. Instead, he said, "Take a closer look around you." The young hunters looked at him impatiently.

"Look closely at those birch trees," Daagoo insisted, and the men stared blankly at the trees. They saw nothing unusual. Daagoo sighed, and this caught the attention of one of the younger men, who tried again to see what the old man saw. Finally, his eyes widened. "Look!" he said, pointing to an empty patch on a birch tree. Then they saw that other trees spaced widely throughout the area had been stripped carefully, almost as if done intentionally so that no one would notice.

"Maybe it was another band," one of the men said.

"Why would they try to hide those empty spots on the trees?" Daagoo asked. The young man shrugged, unable to find an answer.

Then Daagoo gave them instructions. "Before we return," he said, "I want to search this area." Before they could protest, the guide pointed them off in different directions. "If you see anything unusual, come right back here and we will go together to see what it is." Tired as they were, the men began their search, although they were sulky and did not believe that the two women still lived.

Meanwhile, Daagoo set out in the direction he believed the two old women might have taken. "If I were afraid to be found by The People who left me to die, I would go this way," he muttered to himself. "It is a senseless direction because it is far from water. But in winter they would not have to rely on the river, so I think they might be this way."

Daagoo walked a long distance into the willows and beneath the tall spruce trees. As he trudged farther and farther over the snow, he felt weary and wondered if he was doing the right thing. How was it possible to believe that two old women could survive when they, The People, barely made it through that winter? Especially those two women. All they did was complain. Even when little children were hungry, the women complained and criticized. Many times,

Daagoo expected someone to silence them, but that had not happened until the day things had gotten out of control. Daagoo began to feel they were on a useless hunt. The two women must have gotten lost and died along the way. Perhaps they had tried to cross the river and drowned.

As Daagoo thought about all of this, he became more doubtful with each negative thought. Then, suddenly, he smelled something. In the crystal-clear winter air, a light scent of smoke drifted past his nose and was gone. Daagoo stood very still as he tried to catch the scent once more, but there was nothing. For a moment, he wondered if it had been his imagination. Perhaps a summer fire nearby had left its lingering smell in the air. Not wanting to believe that, the old man backtracked slowly until once again he caught the scent. It was a light smell, but this time Daagoo knew that it was no remnant of a summer fire. No, this smoke had a freshness about it. Excited, he tried walking first in one direction, then another until the smoke grew stronger. Convinced that it came from a campfire nearby, his face crinkled into a broad grin as a certainty filled him — the two women had survived.

Daagoo hurried back to get the young men who were waiting as impatiently as before. They did not want to follow when he beckoned, but reluctantly, they followed Daagoo into the night for what seemed a long time. Finally, the guide held out his hand signaling them to stop. Lifting his nose, he told them to smell the air. The hunters sniffed but did not smell anything. "What is it you want us to smell?" one of them asked.

"Just keep smelling," Daagoo answered, so the men sniffed the air again until one exclaimed, "I smell smoke!" The others walked around sniffing the air with more interest now until they, too, smelled it. Still skeptical, one of the younger men asked Daagoo what he expected to find. "We will see," he said simply as he led them farther toward the smoke.

The guide's eyes strained into the darkness

looking for the light of a campfire. He saw nothing but outlines of spruce trees and willows. Aided by the small lights of the many stars above, Daagoo saw that the snow was untrampled. Everything was still and quiet. Yet, the evidence of smoke told him that somewhere near someone was camping. As sure as the blood raced through his veins, the old tracker was now confident that the two old women were alive and at that moment, close. He could not contain his excitement, turning to the younger men and saying, "The two old women are near." Chills ran down the spines of the younger men. They still did not believe that the old ones had survived.

Cupping his hands to his mouth, Daagoo called the women's names into the velvet night and identified himself. Then he waited, hearing only the sound of his own words swallowed by the silence.

CHAPTER 7
The stillness is broken

Ch'idzigyaak and Sa' had settled down for the night. As usual, after doing their daily chores and eating their supper, the two women sat and talked over their fire. They spoke more of The People these days. Loneliness and time had healed their most bitter memories, and the hate and fear born from last year's unexpected betrayal seemed to have been numbed by the many nights they spent sitting and listening to their own thoughts. It all seemed like a distant dream. Now, with their bellies full, the women found themselves in the comfort of their shelter speaking of how much they missed The People. When they ran out of conversation, the women sat silently, each wrapped in her own thoughts.

Suddenly, out of the stillness, the women heard their names called. From across the campfire, their eyes met, and they knew what they heard was not their imagination. The man's voice became loud, and he identified himself. The women knew the old guide. Perhaps they could trust him. But what of the others? It was Ch'idzigyaak who spoke first. "Even if we do not answer, they will find us."

Sa' agreed. "Yes, they will find us," she said as her mind raced with many thoughts.

"What will we do?" Ch'idzigyaak whined in panic.

Sa' took a while to think. Then she said, "We must let them know we are here." Seeing the look of hysteria enter her friend's eyes, Sa' hastened to say in smooth, confident tones, "We must be brave and face them. But, my friend, be prepared for anything." She waited a moment before she added, "Even death." This did not comfort Ch'idzigyaak, who looked as frightened as her friend ever had seen her.

The two women sat a long time trying to gather what courage they had left. They knew they could run no longer. Finally, Sa' got up slowly and went outside into the cold night air, hollering rather hoarsely, "We are here!"

Daagoo had been standing patiently, alertly, while the young hunters eyed him in doubt. What if it were someone else? An enemy perhaps? Just as one of the men was about to voice doubts, out of the darkness they heard Sa' answer. The old guide's face broke into a wide smile. He knew it! They were alive. Immediately, they headed in the direction of the sound. The cold air made the woman's voice seem close, but it took the men some time to reach the camp.

Finally, the men approached the light of the campfire that had been built outside the shelter. Standing by it were the two old women armed with long, sharp, dangerous-looking spears. Daagoo had to smile in admiration of the old women who stood like two warriors ready to defend themselves. "We mean you no harm," he assured them.

The women stared at him defiantly a moment before Sa' said, "I believe you come in peace. But why are you here?" The guide stood a moment, unsure how to explain himself. "The chief sent me here to find you. He believed you were alive and told us to find you."

"Why?" Ch'idzigyaak asked suspiciously.

"I do not know," Daagoo said simply. Indeed, he was surprised to find that he did not know what he or the chief thought would happen once they found the two women, for it was obvious that the women did not trust him or the other men. "I will have to return to the chief to report that we have found you," he said. The two

J. L. Grant

women knew this. "What then?" Sa' asked.

The guide shrugged. "I do not know. But the chief will protect you no matter what happens."

"Like he did the last time?" Ch'idzigyaak asked sharply.

Daagoo knew that if he wanted to, he and the three hunters easily could overtake these two women and their weapons. Yet, he felt his admiration grow stronger because the two women were ready to fight whatever they had to face. These were not the same women he had known before.

"You have my word," he said quietly, and the women could feel the magnitude of what he said as they stood still a long time.

Sa' noticed how worn and weary the men looked. Even the guide who stood proudly had a destitute look about him. "You look tired," she said in a grudging tone. "Come inside," and she led them into their spacious and warm shelter.

The four men entered the tent cautiously, knowing that they were not welcome guests. The women motioned them to sit down, and after the men were seated around the warm fire, Sa' dug around in the back of her bedding along the tent wall and pulled out a fishbag, handing a portion of dried fish to each of the men. As the men ate the fish, they looked around. They could see that the women's bedding was made of newly woven rabbit fur. The two women looked to be in better shape than The People. How could that be? After the men ate their dried fish, Sa' served them boiled rabbit broth, which they drank gratefully.

Meanwhile, Ch'idzigyaak sat to the side staring rather balefully at the hunters, making them feel uncomfortable. With astonishment, the men realized these two women not only had survived but also sat before them in good health while they, the strongest men of the band, were half-starved.

Sa' also stared at the men as they ate their food. She noticed that they tried to eat slowly, but now that they were in the light, she could tell from their lean faces that they had not been eating well. Ch'idzigyaak noticed this, too, but her heart was filled with resentment at this unwanted intrusion, and she did not feel pity. When the men finished their food, Daagoo looked at the women expectantly as he waited for them to say something.

For a while no one broke the silence. Finally, Daagoo said, "The chief believed that you survived, so he sent us to find you." Ch'idzigyaak let out an angry grunt, and when the men turned to her, she gave them a mean look and turned her face away. She could not believe that these people had the nerve to search for them. Surely Sa' could see that they were up to no good. Sa' reached out and patted her friend's hand consolingly, then turned to the men and said simply, "Yes, we have survived."

Daagoo's mouth twitched in amusement at Ch'idzigyaak's wrath. Yet Sa' seemed not to hold too much of a grudge, so he avoided the glaring eyes of Ch'idzigyaak and spoke to Sa' instead. "We are starving, and the cold gets worse. Again we have little food, and we are in the same shape as when we left you. But when the chief hears you are well, he will ask you to come back to our group. The chief and most of The People feel as I do. We are sorry for what was done to you."

The women sat silently a long time. Finally Sa' said, "So you may leave us alone once more just when we need you the most?" Daagoo took a few minutes to respond, wishing the chief was there to answer, for the chief was more experienced in answering such questions.

"I cannot say that it will not happen again.

In hard times, some grow meaner than wolves, and others grow scared and weak, like I did when you were left behind." Daagoo's voice filled with sudden emotion at those last words, but he steadied his voice and continued. "I can tell you one thing right now. If it ever does happen again, I will protect you with my own life as long as I live." As he spoke, Daagoo realized that in these two women, whom he once thought of as helpless and weak, he had rediscovered the inner strength that had deserted him the winter before. Now, somehow, he knew that he never would believe himself to be old and weak again. Never!

The younger men had sat quietly and listened to the exchange between their elders. Now, one of them spoke out in a youthfully passionate voice, "I, too, will protect you if anyone ever tries to do you harm again." Everyone looked at him in surprise. Then his peers also vowed to protect the two women, for they had been witness to a miraculous survival and had regained a stronger sense of respect for the old ones. The women could feel their hearts soften at these words. Still, there was distrust, for, though they believed these men, the women were unsure about the others.

The two women huddled together for a private conference. "Can we trust them?" Ch'idzigyaak asked. Sa' paused a moment, then nodded her head and said softly, "Yes."

"What of the other people? What if they knew of our caches? Do you think they will hold back when they see all our food? Look how hungry these men are. Last year they did not respect us. Here you are willing to let them come to us! My friend, I fear that they will take our food from us whether we like it or not," Ch'idzigyaak said. Sa' already had thought of this, but she was not afraid. Instead, she answered, "We have to remember that they are suffering. Yes, they were too quick to condemn us, but now we have proven them wrong. If they do the same thing, we both know that we can survive. We have proven that much to ourselves. Now we must put aside our pride long enough to remember that they are suffering. If not for the adults, then for the children. Could you forget your own grandson?"

Ch'idzigyaak knew her friend was right, as usual. No, she could not be so selfish as to let her grandson go hungry when she had so much food to eat. The men waited patiently as the two women whispered between themselves.

Sa' was not through talking, for she knew that Ch'idzigyaak still harbored fear about what was happening and needed confidence to face the future. "They do not know we have done well for ourselves," she said. "But tomorrow in the daylight they will see, and then we will know if what they say is true. But remember this, my friend. If they do the same to us again, we will survive. And if they truly mean what they say, then maybe we will always be a reminder to them in harder times ahead."

Ch'idzigyaak nodded in agreement. For a

moment, seeing these members of the band, she felt her old fears and forgot her renewed strength. She looked at her friend with great fondness. Sa' always seemed to know the right thing to say.

In the shelter that night, the two women and the guide exchanged stories while the younger men sat in respectful and attentive silence. The old man told all that had happened after The People left the two women behind. He spoke of the ones who had died. Most were children. Unshed tears glistened in the old women's eyes as they listened, for they had loved some of these people, and the children were among their favorites. The women could not bear to think of how much the children might have suffered before they died so young and so cruelly.

After Daagoo finished his story, Sa' told him how they survived. The men sat with mixed emotions. The story she told sounded unbelievable, yet the women's very presence was evidence of its truth. Sa' did not mind the look of awe she saw in the men's faces. She continued telling her story as she looked back into the eventful year she and Ch'idzigyaak had shared. When she ended her story by telling them of their many food caches, their visitors' eyes became alert.

"When we heard your voice the first time, we knew we could trust you. We also knew that since you were able to find us in the night, it would take little time for you to find our food caches, too. That is why I am telling you now. We know you mean us no harm." Sa' spoke directly to Daagoo. "But what of The People? If they can do such a thing as leave us behind, then they will have no feelings about taking what is ours. They will think of us again as weak and old with no need for our large caches. I do not blame them now for what they have done to us, for my friend and I know what hunger can do to a person. But we have worked hard for what we have, and though we knew it would be too much for us to eat during the winter, we stored it anyway. Maybe it was because we thought this might happen." Sa' paused to consider her words carefully. Then she added, "We will share with The People, but they must not become greedy and try to take our food, for we will fight to our deaths for what is ours."

The men sat in silence listening to Sa' speak in a strong and passionate voice. Then she laid down their terms: "You will stay at the old camp. We do not wish to see anyone else but you," Sa' motioned to Daagoo, "and the chief. We will give you food, and we hope The People will eat sparingly in knowledge of harder times to come. This is all we can do for you." The guide nodded in acknowledgement and said in a quiet voice, "I will return with this message to the chief."

After they said all that had to be said, the women invited the men to sleep on one side of the shelter. For the first time in a long time, the women felt themselves relax. In those long months they feared many things. Now their visions of wolves and other predators faded away, and the women fell into a worry-free sleep.

They were no longer alone.

CHAPTER 8
A new beginning

*B*efore the men left the next day, the women packed large bundles of dry fish, enough to restore The People's energy for travel. Meanwhile, the chief waited anxiously. He feared that something had happened to his men, yet hope kept intruding on that thought. When the men returned, the chief quickly gathered the council to hear their story.

The guide told the stunned people what

they had discovered. When he finished his story, he told them that the women did not trust them and did not want to see them. Daagoo told them of the terms the women had set. After a few minutes of silence, the chief said, "We will respect the women's wishes. Anyone who disagrees will have to fight me."

Daagoo was quick to join in, "The young men and I will stand by you." The council members who had suggested abandoning the two old women were deeply ashamed. Finally, one of them spoke. "We were wrong to leave them behind. They proved it so. Now we will pay them back with respect."

After the chief announced the news to all, The People agreed to follow the rules set by the two women. After their energy was restored by the nourishing dried fish, The People began to pack, for they could not wait to see the two women. In this time of hardship the news of their survival filled the band with a sense of hope and awe. Ch'idzigyaak's daughter, Ozhii Nelii, wept when she heard the news. She had believed her mother to be dead but knew, despite her own overwhelming relief, that her mother would never forgive her. Shruh Zhuu was so ecstatic that, when he heard the news, the young boy immediately gathered his things and was ready to go.

It took the band quite a while to reach the camp where the bark had been stripped off the birch trees. The chief and Daagoo had gone ahead to meet with the two women, and when they arrived at the women's camp, the chief had to contain himself from embracing them. The women eyed him with distrust, so they all sat down to talk instead. The women told the chief what they expected from The People. He responded by telling them their wishes would be obeyed. "We will give you enough food for The People, and when it becomes low, we will give you more food. We will give you small portions at a time," Sa' told the chief, who nodded his head almost humbly.

It took another day before the band reached

the new camp, unpacked and set up tents. Then the chief and his men arrived with bundles of fish and rabbit-fur clothing. Daagoo had hinted boldly to the old women of the poor condition of the band's clothing after he spotted their large collection of rabbit-fur garments. The women both knew they never would use the many mittens, head coverings, blankets and vests they had made in their spare time, so they felt obligated to share with those who needed them. After The People settled down in their new camp and their bellies no longer cried for nourishment, they became more curious about the two old women. But they were forbidden to go near that camp.

The colder days came and stayed a long time, and The People carefully rationed the food that the old women shared. Then the hunters killed a large moose and hauled it many miles back to the camp where all rejoiced at the good fortune.

All this time the chief and the guide took turns making daily visits to the women. When it became apparent that the two women also were curious about The People, the chief asked permission for others to visit, too. Ch'idzigyaak was quick to say no, for her pride was the strongest. But later, the two women talked about it and admitted to themselves that they were ready for visitors. This was especially so for Ch'idzigyaak, who missed her family terribly. When the chief arrived the next day, the two women told him of their decision, and soon people began visiting. At first they were timid and unsure. But after a few visits, they all talked more easily, and soon laughter and light-hearted chatter could be heard from inside the shelter. Each time the visitors came, they brought the two women gifts of moosemeat or animal furs, which the women accepted gratefully.

Relations became better between The People and the two women. Both learned that from hardship, a side of people emerged that they had not known. The People had thought themselves to be strong, yet they had been weak. And the two old ones whom they thought to be the most helpless and useless had proven themselves to be strong. Now, an unspoken understanding existed between them, and The People found themselves seeking out the company of the two women for advice and to learn new things. Now they realized that because the two women had lived so long, surely they knew a lot more than The People had believed.

Visitors came and went daily from the women's camp. Long after they left, Ch'idzigyaak would stand and stare after them. Sa' watched her and felt pity for her friend, for she knew that Ch'idzigyaak expected to see her daughter and grandson, but they did not come. Ch'idzigyaak harbored a secret fear in her heart that perhaps something bad had happened to them and The People did not want to tell her, but she was afraid to ask.

One day, as Ch'idzigyaak gathered wood, a young voice behind her said softly, "I have come for my hatchet." Ch'idzigyaak stood slowly and the wood in her arms fell unnoticed to the ground as she turned. They stared at each other, almost as if they were in a dream and could not believe what they saw. Faces wet with tears, Ch'idzigyaak and her grandson stared at each other in happiness, and no words seemed worth speaking at that moment. Without further hesitation, Ch'idzigyaak reached out to embrace this young boy whom she loved.

Sa' stood by smiling at the happy reunion. The young boy looked up to see Sa' and went over to her and gave her a gentle hug. Sa' felt her heart swell with love and pride for this youngster.

Still, Ch'idzigyaak wondered about her daughter. Despite all that had happened, Ch'idzigyaak yearned to see her own flesh and blood. Being the observant one, Sa' knew this was why her friend seemed sad despite their good fortune. One day after another of the grandson's visits, Sa' reached over and grasped her friend's hand. "She will come," she said simply, and Ch'idzigyaak nodded her head, although she did not quite believe it.

Winter was almost over. A well-trodden path lay between the two camps. The People could not get enough of the women's company, especially the children, who spent many hours laughing and playing in the camp while the old women sat beside their shelter and watched. They were grateful to have survived to witness this. No longer did they take each day for granted.

The young grandson came every day. He helped his grandmothers with their daily chores as before and listened to their stories. One day, the older woman could wait no longer and finally found the courage to ask, "Where is my daughter? Why does she not come?" The young boy answered honestly. "She is in shame, grandmother. She thinks that you have hated her since that day when she turned her back on you. She has cried every day since we parted," the young boy said as he put his arms around her. "I am worried about her, for she is making herself old with grief."

Ch'idzigyaak sat listening, and her heart went out to her daughter. Yes, she had been very angry. What mother would not be? For all those years she trained her daughter to be strong, only to find the training had been for nothing. Yet, Ch'idzigyaak thought to herself, she is not to be blamed for everything. After all, everyone had participated, and her daughter had acted out of fear. She had been frightened for her son's and mother's lives. It was as simple as that. Ch'idzigyaak also acknowledged that her daughter had been brave to leave the bundle of babiche with the two women. To have left a thing of such value with old ones thought to be near death would have been seen as a foolhardy waste.

Yes, she could forgive her daughter. She could even thank her, for she decided that had it not been for the babiche, they might not have survived. Ch'idzigyaak broke out of her thoughts as she realized that her grandson waited for her to say something. Putting her arms around his shoulders, she patted him gently and said, "Tell my daughter that I do not hate her, grandson." Relief flooded the boy's face, for he had spent months worrying about his mother and grand-mother. Now, everything was almost the way it once was. Without further encouragement, the boy gave his grandmother an exuberant hug before he bolted out of the shelter and ran all the way home.

He arrived at the camp breathless. Bursting in on his mother, the excited youth said in be-tween gasps, "Mother! Grandmother wishes to see you! She told me there are no hard feelings!"

Ozhii Nelii was stunned. She had not expected this, and for a moment her legs became so weak that she had to sit down. Her body trembled, and she looked once more at her son. "Is this true?" she asked. "Yes," Shruh Zhuu replied, and his mother saw that he spoke the truth.

At first, she was afraid to go, for she still felt guilty. But at her son's gentle insistence, Ozhii Nelii gathered enough courage to take the long walk to her mother's camp with her son at her side. When they arrived, the two old women were standing outside the shelter, talking. Sa' saw the visitors first, then Ch'idzigyaak turned to see what caused Sa's silence. When she saw her daughter, her mouth opened but words would not come out. Instead, the women stared at each other until Ch'idzigyaak walked to Ozhii Nelii and embraced her tightly, weeping. All that had stood between them seemed to vanish with the touch.

Sa' stood with her arms around Shruh Zhuu, tearfully watching mother and daughter find the love they thought was lost forever. Then Ch'idzigyaak turned and walked into the tent, returning with a small bundle that she pressed into her daughter's hands. Ozhii Nelii saw that it was babiche. She did not understand until Ch'idzigyaak leaned forward and whispered something into her daughter's ear. Ozhii Nelii looked surprised a moment, then she, too, smiled. Again the women fell into one another's arms and embraced.

After everyone had been reunited, the chief appointed the two women to honorary positions within the band. At first, people wanted to help the old ones in any way they could, but the women would not allow too much assistance, for they enjoyed their newly found independence. So The People showed their repect for the two women by listening to what they had to say.

More hard times were to follow, for in the cold land of the North it could be no other way, but The People kept their promise. They never again abandoned any elder. They had learned a lesson taught by two whom they came to love and care for until each died a truly happy old woman.

About the Gwich'in People

The people Velma Wallis has written about in *Two Old Women* are part of the Gwich'in band that roamed the area around what is now Fort Yukon and Chalkyitsik, one of eleven distinct Athabascan groups in Alaska. The Gwich'in people are found in the western interior of the state along the Yukon, Porcupine and Tanana rivers.

While each group has its own dialect, many Alaskan Athabascans not only are able to understand the language of other bands but also share language roots with the Navajo and Apache tribes. All are believed to have descended from Asians who crossed from eastern Siberia into Alaska during an early Ice Age.

The Athabascans are distributed throughout interior Alaska, most of them living between the Brooks Range and the Alaska Range. Those living on the major river systems have relied on the annual salmon runs for subsistence, while tribes farther inland — such as the Gwich'in people — also depend heavily on large game such as moose and caribou and small animals such as rabbits and squirrels.

Historically, each of Alaska's Athabascan groups had a traditional territory. The hunters of each group were well familiar with their terrritory, in part because it was considered dangerous to travel through the territory of other groups. Each territory delineated the hunting and fishing domain of the group. Encroachment into another's territory was rare, and when it did occur, it usually invited violence.

The mobility of the Athabascans was naturally due to their lifestyle of following the resources. They could not afford to sit around and wait for the resources to come to them; such negligence invited hunger and starvation. So they moved around, establishing camps at places which predictably yielded good hunting or fishing according to the season.

Athabascans sometimes faced times of starvation because the land was unable to produce enough for them. While not necessarily a daily threat to existence, the possibility of starvation was a well-known fact of life. People worked hard. The boreal forest was not an easy place to make a living. Life was comprised of many tasks and duties, which, if not performed, may have led to disaster.

By 1900, the Athabascan people began to settle in more permanent camps or villages. This was a result of such factors as population declines brought on by disease, involvement in the fur trade, access to trading posts, and, later, enforced school attendance. Even today, although many people work at wage labor and actively partici-pate in the market economy, subsistence — living off the land — continues to be a vital component of life for most Alaskan Athabascans.

Editor's Afterword

Over the years I'd heard the legend of the two old women in nearly every Athabascan village along the Yukon River, but I'd never given it much thought until Velma Wallis's powerful manuscript brought the story to life.

Too often, living off the land is romanticized, but in *Two Old Women,* Wallis tells it like it is. No matter how skilled a hunter or fisherman might be, subsistence living is a gamble. Starvation can result from the slightest whim of nature such as the failure of a salmon run, an early freeze that kills a generation of migratory birds, or crippling snows that decimate the moose population.

Wallis and those whose experiences she'd drawn on had been there. They researched this book with their stomachs.

Wallis sent her manuscript to Epicenter Press in 1989. Barely a year old, Epicenter lacked the funds to publish this book but strongly believed that it should be published. So, without consulting Wallis, I made the rounds of Native organizations that might back the project. The idea was rejected universally. Wallis was an unknown female with no powerful Native backers. All agreed that Wallis was a promising writer. The problem was that the story she'd chosen to tell was too realistic in dealing with the grim politics of famine. "It makes Athabascan people look bad," one Native leader told me flatly.

The project languished. I explained the situation to Wallis, and she understood. She'd heard the same reaction from some Athabascans in Fort Yukon. "Sometimes I feel like Salman Rushdie — decidedly unpopular," she said.

Six months later, Athabascan Marilyn Savage, a student from Fort Yukon taking my writing class at the University of Alaska Fairbanks, asked me, "Whatever happened to Velma's book?"

I described the obstacles, including a threat to blow up my home if Epicenter published the book. My group of writers grew quiet. Then, almost as an aside, I said, "You know, I'd gladly pay $200 of my own money to see that book in print."

"So would I!" Savage declared. "So would I," echoed other students in the class.

"That's how books originally were published, by subscription," student Steve Rice reminded us.

We decided to go for it. Word spread. By the time $2,000 was committed, Epicenter Press had found the funds to publish the book without help. But it's doubtful the book would have been published without the original backing of the Wallis "subscribers." In early 1992, Wallis flew to Fairbanks from Fort Yukon for the author's first conference with her editor, arriving with a low-keyed self assurance that made me like her immediately. She was quiet — not shy, but careful in her choice of words. English was her first language, but she spoke it accented with the slightly rolled edges that makes the Athabascan dialects so charming. And so was she. At thirty, she was in love for the first time and hoping to have a child. The finished manuscript and Velma Wallis's daughter, Laura Brianna, were delivered about the same time. Laura Brianna arrived with a slight case of jaundice — easily cured. And the manuscript had just one minor glitch.

"Did I tell you about the commas?" the author had asked as she grew more comfortable in dealing with her editor. "Although I got my GED, I've always had trouble with commas. I know most sentences have them but I didn't know where to put them, so I'd write up the story and just sprinkle a few in. Finally, my brother Barry said, 'Velma, why don't you take them out entirely until you figure it out — maybe someone will help you!'"

The mental picture of Velma Wallis with a paper shaker full of commas, seasoning her story, still makes me smile. By the time she completed her second book, *Bird Girl*, she didn't need much help. But we'd gladly put in commas all day for Wallis, just for the opportunity to read her stories , , , , , , ,

Lael Morgan

Book Club Discussion Guide

In her memoir, *Raising Ourselves,* Velma Wallis talks about struggling to understand her people's past while at the same time trying to come to grips with their unknown future. Drugs and alcohol are problems that she deals with in her community. Disease has had a devastating impact on the Native population as well. "I almost believed that drinking and drugs were all we as Native people had ever been about until that day when my mother first told me the story about the two old women." This is the story that helped to shape her future. By hearing stories from her people's past she discovered that they were strong, resilient, and above all, had reason to hope. "I saw hope that we could still be the people we once were, not in the literal sense, but possessing the same pride that our ancestors had before the epidemics and cultural changes."

The popularity of *Two Old Women* surprised the author, whose success was met with mixed reviews in her Native community. Some of the elders thought that she was telling stories to an audience for whom they were not intended, thus violating the tribe's privacy. However, others believed that the adaptation would be good for the Gwich'in people because it kept their past alive, and gained some exposure for their people. The stories are part of the Gwich'in identity, and by publishing the legend, Wallis has done her part preserving the collective memories of her people.

In the author's introduction, she explains that although she has used her imagination to embellish the story, the true essence of the legend is left unchanged. "This story told me that there is no limit to one's ability — certainly not age — to accomplish in life what one must. Within each individual in this large and complicated world there lives an astounding potential of greatness. Yet it is rare that these hidden gifts are brought to life unless by the chance of fate."

Once published, the story of *Two Old Women* took on a life of its own, and many interpretations have emerged. The universal themes of respect for the elderly, empowering women, and the strength of the human will are addressed among other issues. Wallis told a reporter she "never, intended *Two Old Women* to mean so many different things." This is the power inherent in stories like this one. They can take on many meanings and hold many truths, sometimes ones that were not envisioned, or even intended by the author.

These questions and discussion topics are offered to enhance your group's reading and discussion of the legend retold by Velma Wallis.

1. "Some are born great, some achieve greatness, and some have greatness thrust upon 'em" (Shakespeare's *Twelfth Night*). How much of

the women's miraculous survival was dependent on fate or luck? How much was based on their will to survive? Their training? Their childhood experiences? What role did the grandson and daughter play in helping the two old women to survive?

2. Why does a legend from a specific tribe in remote Alaska resonate among readers worldwide? What universal truths exist in this story? What does this story say about growing old? What does it say about the role of women in this ancient society? Does this have implications for modern society?

3. The practice of leaving older or weaker individuals behind in times of severe hunger was not uncommon in many nomadic traditions. Was the practice justifiable to ensure the survival of the group? What role does tradition play in the story? How does that relate to age and gender? What traditions are changed in

the end? What implications does the now abandoned practice have for modern society?

4. How did the old women change in the year from their abandonment to their rediscovery? What kept them going? Was it spite? Pride? Love? A strong will to live? Did the old women want to live, so that ultimately they could meet death on their own terms? What is meant by "Let us die trying?"

5. Velma Wallis in her introduction says that legends and stories "are gifts given by an elder to a younger person." The two abandoned women share stories from their childhood with each other. How do they use these stories to help them survive? What does this say, if anything, about the power and importance of stories? Why are they gifts?

6. Whom do you most identify with in the story? The two old women? The People? Others?

Whom do you feel sorry for, if anyone? How does the author tell the story in such a way that we feel sorry for the two old women, but also for The People as well? Is this an important aspect of the story?

Author Velma Wallis with her mother, Mae Wallis, and daughter, Laura Brianna, in Fort Yukon, Alaska, shortly before the first edition of Two Old Women was published in 1993.

Velma Wallis

The author, 44, was born in Fort Yukon, a remote community with a population of about 650 people just upriver from the confluence of the Yukon and Porcupine rivers in northwest Alaska. Reachable only by airplane, dog sled, snow machine, or riverboat, Fort Yukon is the largest village in the Yukon Flats, a vast fur-trapping region of nearly 10 million acres known for the state's widest temperature swings — a record low of 71° F below zero and an all-time high of 97°.

One of thirteen children, Wallis was raised in a family that adhered to her people's traditional values. She was thirteen when her father died and she dropped out of school to help her mother raise her younger brothers and sisters. After her siblings became independent, she passed her high school equivalency exam, then moved to a trapping cabin twelve miles from fort Yukon, living off the land, intermittently for a dozen years by hunting, fishing, and trapping.

Wallis has written two other books, *Bird Girl & the Man Who Followed the Sun* and *Raising Ourselves: A Gwich'in Coming of Age Story from the Yukon River*.

James Grant

James Grant Sr. was born in the Athabascan village of Tanana, Alaska in 1946, and raised in California. He attended Chaffey Junior College in Alta Loma, California, and the University of Alaska in Fairbanks, where he now lives. While stationed in Europe with the U.S. Army, Grant had an opportunity to travel and to study the masters. His art also included mask making, wood and ivory carving, bronze casting, oil painting, and pen and ink.

Recommendations for readers interested in learning more about Alaska's Native people:

ART & ESKIMO POWER
The life and times of Alaskan Howard Rock
Lael Morgan
$16.95 paperback

BIRD GIRL & THE MAN WHO FOLLOWED THE SUN
Velma Wallis
$19.95 hardbound

COLD RIVER SPIRITS
Legacy of an Athabascan-Irish family from Alaska's Yukon River
Jan Harper-Haines
$19.95 hardbound

RAISING OURSELVES
A Gwich'in Coming of Age Story from the Yukon River
Velma Wallis
$14.95 paperback

SEVEN WORDS FOR WIND
Essays and Field Notes from Alaska's Pribilof Islands
Sumner MacLeish
$16.95 hardbound

SPIRIT OF THE WIND
The Story of George Attla, legendary sled dog sprint champion
Lew Freedman
$14.95 paperback

TUNDRA TEACHER
A memoir of teaching school, and learning about life, in rural Alaska
John Foley
$14.95 paperback

These titles from Epicenter Press may be found at or special-ordered from your local bookstore. They also may be ordered online at www.EpicenterPress.com or by phoning toll-free to our 24-hour order line, 800-950-6663. Or mail payment (Visa, MC accepted) to: PO Box 82368, Kenmore, WA 98028. Add $6 shipping/handling for one or two books, $8 for three or more. WA residents add 8.8% state sales tax.